ABOUT TH

Christopher Pike was born in New York, but grew up in Los Angeles, where he still lives. Prior to becoming a writer he worked in a factory, painted houses and programmed computers. His hobbies include astronomy, meditating, running and making sure his books are prominently displayed in his local bookshop. As well as being a best-selling children's writer, he is also the author of three adult novels.

Spooksville

Spooksville

THE EVIL HOUSE

Christopher Pike

Hodder
Children's
Books

a division of Hodder Headline plc

One

Halloween night in Spooksville.

What could be more perfect?

Well . . . many things.

The gang was gathered at Bryce Poole's house, and
of course no one else was home except Bryce because
he said his home was his *own*. The gang did not
necessarily believe him but it was a fact that the house
looked as if only one person lived there. There was
only one bed in each bedroom, and only one set of
clothes in each wardrobe. But after all the gang had
gone through the previous summer, they were not
easily impressed.

Outside it was getting dark and pumpkins were
beginning to glow and there was still discussion going
on about what they were going to be for Halloween. The
main problem was that Bryce had decided to be a

vampire while Sally Wilcox already had on a vampire costume. That was not a problem for Bryce, but for Sally it was a disaster of major proportions.

'People will think we are brother and sister,' Sally complained as she stood before a mirror in the living room and darkened her eyelashes. Sally naturally had dark hair, but with her long black cape and ghoulish make-up, she looked like an awesome vampire. She had even coloured her tongue purple, which was a nice effect, and had fake blood dripping out of the side of her heavily-painted lips.

'You should be so lucky,' replied Bryce, who was an even more imposing vampire than Sally. His black cape was made of real leather and the stark white of his face looked more natural – for a vampire that is. With his implanted fangs and red contact lenses he was a truly frightening creature. Of course he was naturally handsome, and that didn't hurt. But it was also the way he moved about the house, as if he might swoop into the air at any moment. He had obviously spent serious time and money preparing for the night and wasn't about to be talked out of being a vampire. Sally whirled in his direction.

'If you want to stay a vampire,' she said, 'you will have to walk behind the rest of us.'

'That's fair,' Cindy Makey said sarcastically, before turning to Bryce. 'I'll walk with you if she won't. At least you look like a real vampire.' Cindy herself was dressed as a fairy princess. Her long blonde hair was tied up beneath a silver crown, and she had two see-through wings spreading gracefully from her back. Her shiny gold dress glimmered in the house lights. The wand in her hand was actually made of cardboard, but covered with silver and gold tin foil it looked real.

'This is Halloween,' Watch said diplomatically. 'We can't have too many vampires.' As he spoke he puffed on a brown pipe that was actually lit and smoking, even though he swore he was not inhaling any of the smoke. Watch was Sherlock Holmes, the famous fictional private detective. He had on a brown tweed suit and wore a brown cap above his thick glasses. For the first time in a long while he was not wearing his four watches, just a single gold watch that fitted in his vest pocket. He took it out and checked the time, and added, 'We'd better get going soon if we're to have a full night.'

'I'll be ready in a minute,' Adam Freeman called from the corner. Even though short and relatively new to town, Adam was the unquestioned leader of

3

the group. But when it came to Halloween night, he was a dismal figure. The last month in school had been busy for him, and he had not had time to prepare a proper costume. For tonight he was simply cutting two holes in a sheet – so he could see – and going as a ghost. The rest of the group – except for Watch – was disappointed by his lack of attention to his costume. Apparently Halloween in Spooksville was much more important than Christmas and Easter put together.

'Why even bother with the sheet?' Sally asked as she finished with her eyelashes. 'Why don't you just put on your dirtiest and bloodiest clothes and go as just another Spooksville casualty?'

'I think he looks like an excellent ghost,' Watch said, still puffing on his pipe. 'You have nothing to be ashamed of, Adam.'

Adam pulled off the white sheet and took the scissors to the holes once more. 'If I could just see better I wouldn't mind,' he said. 'I think I'll have to make these holes bigger.'

'Too big and they'll see your face,' Cindy warned.

Sally laughed. 'And that might scare them more than anything.'

Bryce continued to swoop around the room with

his long black cape. 'Are we going to try to do any mischief tonight?' he asked.

'What do you mean?' Cindy asked, a bit uneasily. She was ordinarily the most conservative one in the group, yet at the same time she had her moments.

'What do you mean what does he mean?' Sally asked. 'This is trick or treat night. We've got to do a few tricks if we're to have any fun at all.'

'Like what?' Adam asked, still fooling with his sheet.

'Last year we did a couple of small tricks,' Watch said.

Sally snorted. 'I wouldn't call turning on all the fire hydrants in town a small trick. That was your idea, Watch, admit it.'

'I only turned them on because the fire department hosed us down when we knocked on their door,' Watch said. 'But you were the one, Sally, who tried to burn down the school.'

'I didn't actually try to burn it down,' Sally said. 'If I had, it wouldn't be standing today. All I did was burn down the apple tree in the courtyard.'

'Why would you burn down a nice tree?' Cindy asked in disgust.

'Because the apples it gave were poisonous,' Sally said matter-of-factly. 'Two kids died last year eating them.' Sally suddenly stopped and rubbed her pale

5

hands together. 'You know what I'd really like to do? Burn down the witch's castle.'

It was Adam's turn to snort. 'I'd like to see you try. It's made of solid rock, and I doubt Ann Templeton would even let you near it.'

'Oh, we'll get near to it tonight,' Bryce said. 'Everybody goes to the witch's castle on Halloween night. She gives away the coolest treats.'

Sally snickered. 'I wouldn't say that. Last year she gave me a miniature guillotine. When I asked her what it was for she said I could use it to do my nails. Can you imagine that?'

'Last year she gave me a crystal ball,' Watch said. 'But she didn't say what it was for, except that one day it would save my life.'

'Maybe you can see the future in it,' Cindy said. But Watch shook his head.

'All I see when I look in it is stars,' he said.

'That sounds cool,' Adam said, throwing his sheet back over his head. 'I'm ready. Let's go to her place first. I think we're going to have a fun night.'

'Fun can be dangerous thing in this town,' Sally said.

Two

Ann Templeton's castle looked spectacular as they approached. Each of the towers was glowing with a different coloured light, and even the water in the most swirled with strange coloured gases. The drawbridge that crossed the moat was lit with not less than a dozen gigantic jack o'lanterns. A couple of the pumpkins were as tall as Adam. But the best thing of all – to Adam – was the fact that Ann Templeton herself was sitting out front dressed as, of course, an evil witch.

She sat in a tall black chair, and wore a black robe and a dark red hat that pointed towards the night sky. Beside her, on the left, simmering with dark green steam, was a boiling black pot, lit from the base with glowing coal and crackling logs. On her other side was a black box, which seemed to be filled with different coloured goodies. She gestured with her hand as they neared the castle but Sally stopped them before they stepped on to the moat. She gestured to the swirling dark waters.

'How do we know she won't try to raise the plank the moment we step on to it?' Sally asked. 'Remember, there are crocodiles in those waters.'

'She likes us,' said Adam, who personally adored Ann Templeton. 'She won't hurt us.'

'She likes you,' Sally said. 'She doesn't like me.'

'Last year she did raise the plank on this one kid, Danny Child,' Watch said. 'He slipped and fell in the water. You could hear his screams a mile away. Of course he had a roll of toilet paper in his bag, and had bragged aloud at school about how he was going to paper the witchs' castle.'

Cindy looked ill. 'Did the crocodiles really eat him alive?'

'They didn't try to teach him to swim,' Sally said.

'But on Halloween night Miss Ann Templeton is usually in a good mood,' Bryce said. 'If we don't say anything that angers her, we should be OK. She has already gestured for us to approach.'

'It's hard for me to say anything without angering people,' Sally complained as they stepped on to the drawbridge.

'Then why don't you keep your mouth shut for once,' Cindy suggested.

'I never thought of that,' Sally replied, as if she meant it.

As they drew closer to Ann Templeton they saw that the big boiling pot on her right side was filled with floating cooked human heads. Some were boiled down to skulls but a few of the heads still had most of their features. Adam thought he recognised a kid from school but couldn't be sure. Naturally this made them all a little hesitant about visiting, but she smiled so wickedly at them that they thought it might be a bigger mistake to turn and flee. Since Adam had had the best luck with her in the past, he stepped to the front of the group and held out his pillow sack. They were all carrying pillow sacks except for Bryce who collected his candy in an attaché case.

'Trick or treat,' Adam said, and there was a quiver in his voice. The steam coming off the pot did indeed smell like cooked human flesh. Ann Templeton smiled again but this time there was a gleam in her eyes, a cold gleam of both white and red light.

'What is it to be Adam?' she asked. 'Do I give you a treat or are you going to try to trick me?'

Adam swallowed and his eyes strayed to the pot. 'I would prefer to get a treat.'

'And if I don't give you one?' she asked.

He shrugged. 'No harm done. We'll just be on our way.'

'Ha!' she said with force. 'But you have already said trick or treat. Do you know that in ancient times that used to be considered a contract of sorts? One or the other had to happen. You stand on ancient soil when you stand at my doorstep. I ask you again, if I don't give you a treat, what kind of trick will you play on me?'

Adam tried to think fast. It was never wise to back down in front of the witch. She loathed weakness. He met her penetrating gaze.

'My trick will be a surprise,' he said. 'But I strongly advise you not to risk it. I only say that as a friend.'

Ann Templeton threw her head back and laughed.

'Very good, Adam!' she said. 'That was a mighty answer.' She turned to the black box on her right, which was filled with an assortment of small coloured objects. 'Now what would you like for a treat?'

Sally whispered in Adam's ear. 'Be careful what you ask for,' she said.

'I heard that,' the witch said as she continued to

10

sort through her box. 'Your turn is next Sally.'

'I haven't said trick or treat,' Sally snapped back. 'I don't have to take a turn if I don't want to.'

'True enough,' the witch said, and flashed Sally a cold smile. But then her attention returned to Adam. 'What would you like?'

Adam resettled his sheet over his head. The eye holes had a tendency to move, making it hard to see. 'What do you have?' he asked.

'Anything you might want. Just name it.'

Adam thought for a moment. 'Well, I really like Mars Bars. Do you have any of those?'

Ann Templeton laughed again, this time softly. Without looking, she reached into her black box and pulled out a Mars Bar and dropped it in Adam's sack.

'I like them as well,' she said, before turning to Bryce. 'Are you feeling brave tonight, Count Dracula?'

Bryce stepped forward and held out his bag. 'Trick or treat,' he said firmly.

She nodded. 'You say that like you mean it. What would you like?'

'A phase enhancer for a portable cyclotron that I am building in my garage,' Bryce said with a straight vampire face. 'Also a Mars Bar.'

Ann Templeton considered. 'I would gladly have given you the phase enhancer, even though I know you would have eventually killed yourself with your cyclotron. But since you asked for two items, and not one as tradition dictates, you just get the Mars Bar.' She reached for her black box.

'But . . .' Bryce started to protest.

The witch paused. 'You wish to argue with me?' she asked, and once again a light flashed deep in her green eyes. Bryce quickly shook his head, and each of them noticed a line of fear on his face.

'I would be very happy with the Mars Bar,' he said.

Ann Templeton gave Bryce the candy and then turned to Watch. 'Why, my favourite sleuth,' she said. 'What can I do for you this evening?'

Watch stepped forward and held open his pillow sack. 'Trick or treat,' he said.

But Ann Templeton sat back in her chair. 'No treats. You're going to have to trick me.'

In response Watch pulled out the laser pistol Adam had wrestled from an alien while the bunch of them were trying to save the world seventy million years in the past. Adam had lent it to Watch last week because Watch said he wanted to figure out what

12

powered it. Now Watch pointed it at the swirling waters of the moat, and the dark shapes that moved beneath the surface.

Watch fired off a shot. There was a flash of red light and an explosion of fiery steam. The creatures in the moat flapped angrily but Watch calmly turned back to Ann Templeton.

'If you don't give me a treat, ma'am,' he said. 'I'm going to have to kill all your crocodiles.'

Ann Templeton appeared taken aback. 'Were you a friend of Danny Child?' she asked curiously.

'Couldn't stand the guy,' Watch replied. 'But I do think your crocodiles are a public menace.' He paused. 'But I am willing to negotiate, ma'am.'

Once again Ann Templeton threw her head back and laughed.

'A wonderful bluff, Watch,' she said. 'Fortunately I know you are too sensitive a soul to hurt a fly. But you played the part well and for that you deserve a treat.' She gestured to her black box. 'Come, what would you like?'

Watch straightened his glasses. 'My eyes have been bothering me again, ma'am. I was wondering if you could give me a stronger pair of glasses. I don't have any money to buy them.'

A look of concern crossed Ann Templeton's face. When she spoke next, it was in a gentle voice. 'I once offered to heal your vision permanently,' she said. 'You turned me down. You were afraid you would not be Watch if you didn't have trouble seeing. Do you still feel that way?'

Watch hesitated. 'I don't know, ma'am. I just know that I am reluctant to ask a miracle from you.'

Ann Templeton nodded slowly, thoughtfully.

'But what's a miracle?' she asked. 'Isn't it ignorance? If you'd never seen someone ride a bike before, and then you saw them for the first time, you might think it was a miracle that they could ride it without falling down. Do you see my point?'

'Yes,' Watch said. 'Your magical powers are not miraculous to you because you know how they work.' He paused. 'But I still think the most I can ask for is a stronger pair of glasses, ma'am.'

Ann Templeton held out her hand. 'Give me the glasses you're wearing.' Watch did so and she rubbed them in her palms, carefully, before handing them back to him. 'Put them back on, tell me how well you can see.'

Watch put them on, and suddenly his face brightened.

'I can see better than ever!' he exclaimed. But then his excitement faltered. 'Is this right?' he asked in a quiet voice. Ann Templeton smiled at his question.

'Your eyes have not been changed, Watch,' she said. 'Only your glasses. Please don't worry about this gift. Just enjoy it.' Then she held out her hand. 'But I want the laser pistol. Kids should not play with guns.'

'But we have only used that gun in self defence,' Bryce protested.

'Now you can use your wits,' Ann Templeton said, and gestured with her hand again. 'The gun, please.'

Watch handed it over without hesitation. 'I think I know how it works,' he said, meaning he might be able to build another one. But Ann Templeton had already turned to Cindy, who was standing near the rear of their group.

'Trick or treat, Cindy?' the witch asked.

Cindy shook her head faintly. 'I'm just out tonight for the candy.'

'But I can give you candy,' Ann Templeton said.

'At what price?' Sally whispered.

Cindy made no move to step forward.

The witch chuckled softly. 'I understand, Cindy. You are afraid, and that is not necessarily a bad thing in this town. But remember this is Halloween night. Strange things happen at this time of year. This very night you might find yourself in a very unusual place. A place where fear can kill you, and only your power can save others. Remember that, Cindy, won't you?' She smiled as she added, 'My fairy princess.'

Cindy spoke uneasily. 'I have heard you give good advice.'

Ann Templeton nodded. 'I give the best advice.'

Three

After leaving the witch's castle, they visited a number of ordinary houses and received an assortment of candy and other goodies. But Adam and Cindy were struck by how many houses had their porch lights off.

'There can't be that many people out this evening,' Adam said.

'Of course they're not out,' Sally said. 'They're just acting like they're not there. Most people are just too scared to answer the door. Why, last year there was this character going around dressed as a werewolf. The only trouble was he wasn't wearing a costume at all. He was a real werewolf, and he slaughtered five families before the night was over.'

'There are no such things as werewolves,' Cindy said plainly.

'Did this young woman walk through last summer with a bag over her head or what?' Sally said. 'In this town there is *everything*.'

'Is it true about the werewolf?' Adam asked Watch and Bryce.

'I wouldn't say he slaughtered the five families,' Watch said. 'I heard he just got fur all over their furniture.'

'And at whatever was in their refrigerators,' Bryce said. 'But I don't think the werewolf ate anyone. Except for maybe the Foster kid.'

'Oh yeah,' Watch said, remembering. 'James Foster did disappear last Halloween. But then, he always hung out with Danny Child. Maybe the crocs got them both.'

Cindy sighed. 'Talk like this makes me want to go home and go to bed.'

'What makes you think, you're safe there?' Sally asked. Then her eyes strayed further up the road and she stopped dead in her tracks. 'Oh no,' she moaned. 'We've turned into Dead Lane. Let's go back.'

To Adam's surprise, Watch and Bryce didn't argue.

'We can go back now,' Watch said.

'No sense in being reckless,' Bryce agreed, also turning away from the street.

'Wait,' Adam said. 'What's wrong with this street? It looks pretty ordinary to me.'

'Adam,' Sally said with exaggerated patience. 'When a street is called Dead Lane, you've got to get a clue. This place deserves its name.'

But Adam was curious. 'Why is this street called that?'

'Because of the Evil House,' Watch said. 'It's located at the end of the block.'

'What's so evil about it?' Cindy asked.

'No one who has ever gone into the house has ever come out,' Bryce said. 'For that reason, even I have not dared venture inside.'

'And we all know how brave Bryce is,' Sally muttered sarcastically.

'But have you guys seen the house from the outside?' Adam asked.

'Sure,' Watch said. 'In the daytime. But none of us have gone near it after dark.'

'But what about all the people who live on this block?' Adam asked.

'No one lives on this block,' Watch said, pointing down the road. 'Notice all the lights are out. That one

19

jack o'lantern you see at the end of the road belongs to the Evil House. You can get a glimpse of the place even from here.'

Sally continued to walk the other way. 'We are not getting any closer to it,' she said.

Adam's curiosity had only increased. 'But there must be somebody inside it, then, if they have put a jack o'lantern out on their porch. Doesn't it make you wonder who they are?'

'We are not sure they are *whos*,' Bryce said. 'They might be *whats*.'

'What?' Cindy asked.

'Nonhuman creatures,' Watch explained.

Sally stopped a little way down the road from them. 'Are you guys coming or what?'

Adam continued to stare in the direction of the house. Watch was right – he could glimpse its outline, but could pick out few details. The house was definitely old, however, and large. The light of the lone jack o'lantern spilled over what looked like a dusty and decaying porch. Really, it looked like the perfect Halloween haunt. Adam took a step in its direction.

'I want to get a better look at it,' he muttered.

Watch caught his arm, surprising Adam.

'It's a bad place,' Watch said in a firm voice. 'And you know how bad things happen in bad places. Leave it alone, Adam.'

Adam was prepared to listen to his friend. He had seldom seen Watch so serious. But another glimpse of the old house at the end of the dead end block stirred a strange longing in him. He suddenly felt as if he *must* get closer to it, as if it drew him somehow. He shook off his friend's grip.

'You guys wait here,' he said. 'I'll only be gone a few minutes.'

'Famous last words in this town,' Sally muttered.

'Adam,' Cindy said, puzzled. 'It's unlike you to go looking for trouble, especially after everything we've been through lately. Listen to Watch, he knows best. Let's just get some more candy and go home.'

But Adam was already walking towards the Evil House.

'It can't hurt me if I'm out on the street,' he said.

The gang followed him. Adam heard them behind him, but didn't bother to turn and say anything. At least not until he was standing near the edge of the Evil House's overgrown front yard. The whole walk towards the house, Adam found he couldn't stop staring at the lit jack o'lantern out front. It was

21

only when he was beside the house that he realized why.

There was a flame in the pumpkin.

But there did not appear to be a candle.

He pointed out that fact as his friend came up behind him.

'How could a flame burn without something to support it?' Adam asked aloud.

'It's impossible,' Bryce said.

'It's bad omen,' Sally said. 'Let's take the hint and get out of here.'

'This house looks hundreds of years old,' Cindy said.

Cindy was not exaggerating. There was hardly a speck of paint left on the wooden beams. Besides being covered with dust, the place was tangled in cobwebs. The odd thing was there were still un-broken glass panes in the windows, and curtains hanging on the other side of them. At least it seemed odd to Adam. He took it as another sign the place was occupied and said as much to the others.

'No one is questioning whether the place is empty or not,' Watch said, putting away his pipe. 'We're just saying the place is dangerous.'

'Don't you want to at least peer in the pumpkin to

see how the flame is hanging in midair?' Adam asked his friend.

Watch paused and stared in the direction of the jack o'lantern with his new and improved glasses. 'I wouldn't mind a peek,' he admitted.

Sally threw a fit. 'No! You guys get up on that porch and you're as good as dead. Bryce, tell them.'

Bryce considered. 'I don't think we're in any immediate danger if we don't actually go in the house.'

'What?' Sally asked him in amazement. 'Are you just saying that because I have treated you like garbage lately or is it because you truly believe it?'

Bryce smiled. 'I think it's a little of both.'

'If we're going to look at it,' Cindy said, shivering in her fairy princess costume, which was not exactly warm, 'then let's do it and get out of here.'

Sally shook her head as they stepped towards the porch.

'We are going to regret this for the rest of short lives,' she muttered.

The porch creaked loudly as they stepped on to it, making them all jump slightly. They waited with their breath held, but no sound came from inside and they moved to the jack o'lantern. Only they could not remove the top of the pumpkin because it had never been cut open. Yet the inside was hollow – they could see the flame clearly through the wickedly grinning mouth. As a group they knelt and stared at it, and nothing changed with a closer look.

The flame was simply floating in mid air.

'Cool,' Watch whispered.

'Cool?' Sally complained. 'It's evil. This whole place is.' She straightened. 'Now I'm getting out of here no matter what you guys say.' She turned for the road, then froze on the spot.

A faint cry sounded from inside.

A cry of pain. Of despair.

They all climbed to their feet and looked at each other.

'What was that?' Cindy gasped.

'We all know what it was,' Bryce said.

'Do we?' Watch said quietly. 'It sounded like a human cry, but an animal cry can often sound the same.'

'I don't think that was no animal,' Adam said.

'You are employing a double negative,' Watch said.

The cry came again. A painful moan.

'That sounds like a young person,' Adam whispered.

24

'It sounds like a young dead person,' Sally hissed. 'It's a ghost. This place must be stuffed with them. I tell you, we have to get out of here.'

'But what if there is someone inside there,' Adam said, still wearing his sheet, 'and they're in pain? We can't just leave them.'

'If they're inside this house they're beyond reach,' Sally said, beginning to get exasperated. 'Don't even think of trying to rescue them.'

'I'm not talking about rescuing anyone,' Adam said. 'I just want to make sure they're OK.' He paused. 'I'm going inside.'

'Adam,' Watch said softly. 'That is probably a bad idea. You don't fully understand the reputation this place has.'

Adam struggled inside. He did take his friend's warning seriously. But the sound of the cry continued to haunt him. There had been so much suffering in it.

'If I just walk away now,' Adam said finally, 'I will be plagued with guilt.'

Sally put her hand on his shoulder and spoke in a quiet voice.

'It's possible the cry is there just to lure us inside,' she said. 'We know for a fact many people have disappeared inside this house. But what we never knew was why anyone ever went in the house in the first place. I think this cry might be the answer.'

'I am not asking you to come with me,' Adam said.

'You know we're not going to let you go alone,' Watch said.

Adam shrugged. 'You guys know me. I can't just walk away. Why don't we at least knock, see if someone answers?'

'OK,' Watch said. 'I just wish we still had that laser pistol.'

Adam stepped to the front door and they gathered behind him. He knocked lightly but got no response. His next knock was harder.

Hard enough to knock the door slightly open.

Inside it looked black as black.

'Hello,' Adam called softly through the three inches of empty space. But once again, no one answered.

'You see,' Sally said. 'They don't want our help.'

From far away, deep in the house, they again heard the cry.

It sounded so pitiful. So overwhelmingly sad.

Adam turned and looked at his friends through the two holes in his sheet.

'I can't believe someone could fake that sound,' he said. 'We have to see if they are OK.'

'I don't want to go in there,' Cindy said. 'I'm sorry, call me a coward if you want. But this place is just too creepy.'

'Coward,' Sally muttered.

'How dare you!' Cindy snapped.

'You just gave us permission to call you one!' Sally shot back.

'Shh,' Bryce said. 'Let's not wake the dead.'

Adam looked at Bryce. 'You really think there are ghosts in here?'

Bryce pulled the door open a few more inches and peered inside. Then he looked over his shoulder at the rest of them.

'I think going in here will be the most dangerous thing we have ever done,' he said. 'But if Adam thinks we have to do it, then I say we give him our full support.'

'Why do I have to be a victim of Adam's excessive compassion?' Sally muttered.

'You can stay outside with me,' Cindy said.

'I would prefer that the girls remained outside,' Watch said.

Sally erupted. 'If the *boys* are going inside, the

girls are going inside. Right, Cindy?'

'Why do I have to be a victim of Sally's excessive feminism?' Cindy muttered. Then she shrugged. 'If we're going inside, then let's do it and get it over with. I would still like to do some more trick or treating before the night's over.'

'I think the treats are definitely over for the night,' Sally said.

They left their bags of candy outside on the porch.

Four

As a group they entered the house. Both Adam and Sally had flashlights, necessary tools when trick or treating in Spooksville at night. The town had few street lights. Quickly Adam and Sally panned what appeared to be a living room with their flashlights, revealing dusty furniture from the last century, tons of spider webs and cracked wall mirrors.

'One thing is for sure,' Watch said. 'No one has been in this room in a long time. Notice the dust – it has not been disturbed.'

Adam pointed towards a hallway at the far end of the room.

'They cry seemed to come from that direction,' he said.

Watch blinked. 'Did you guys see that?'

'I didn't see anything,' Adam said.

'There was a flash of white light at the end of the hallway,' Watch said.

'The beam of Adam's flashlight probably bounced off a mirror,' Sally said.

'Or else you just saw a ghost,' Cindy said.

'You can't believe in ghosts if you don't believe in werewolves,' Sally said.

'Let's see what's there,' Adam said, leading them slowly forward.

The hallway was long and dark. Numerous rooms led away from it: bedrooms, dens, even a ruined kitchen. Everywhere there was dirt and more cobwebs, yet there was no sign of why the house had been suddenly abandoned.

Near the end of the hallway, where Watch thought he saw his flash of light, they came to what was clearly a kid's bedroom. Stepping inside, they saw several magic show and carnival posters pinned to the peeling walls. At the end of a narrow bed was a large closed wooden chest. On a cracked mirror above a splintered chest of drawers hung a family photograph. It was black and white, extremely faded, and had obviously been taken with primitive equipment. Watch picked it up while the rest of them studied the photo by looking over his shoulder.

There was a man and wife, both dressed like rich people from the previous century. They stood in front of the Evil House, but a much earlier version of it. The place was immaculate. Beside them stood a small, dark-haired boy who wore a T-shirt bearing the inscription:

MARVIN THE MAGNIFICENT

'This must be Marvin's bedroom,' Watch said, glancing around. 'Obviously he was into magic and carnivals.'

'But it looks like Marvin and his family were the last ones to live here,' Cindy said. 'And a long time ago. Who lit the pumpkin outside?'

The Evil House responded.

They heard the pitiful cry again.

It seemed to come from right behind them.

They whirled round but there was no one there.

'Did you see that?' Bryce exclaimed.

'I didn't see anything,' Adam said.

'Neither did I,' Sally said. 'Quit trying to scare us, Bryce.'

'I saw what Watch did,' Bryce said. 'A glimpse of white light. It was about as big as one of us.'

'There's a mirror on the other side of the room as well,' Sally said. 'You just saw our reflected flashlight beam, like Watch.'

'No,' Bryce said confidently. 'I turned quicker than you guys. Your beams weren't even pointed in that direction. Also, this light was unlike any light I've ever seen before.'

'Was it kind of hazy?' Watch asked. 'Kind of swirling like it was alive?'

'Exactly,' Bryce said.

Adam pointed at the chest at the foot of the bed. It had been closed when they had entered the room but now the top was cracked open and a faint red light spilled out from it.

'Look at that,' Adam gasped.

'Maybe the ghost opened it,' Watch said.

'Would you stop that,' Sally said angrily.

'I thought you believed in ghosts,' Cindy said.

'I prefer not to believe in ones that might be in the same house as me,' Sally said.

Adam stepped forward and knelt beside the chest. Watch crouched by his side, and together they eased the top of the chest up. The red light expanded and filled the entire room with an eerie glow. Yet even with the lid off the chest, they could not see where the light was coming from, not exactly. It just seemed to radiate from the bottom of the chest. Watch reached into the chest and pulled out a purple cloak and a pack of playing cards. Only the cards were trick cards, the kind used by magicians. There were other pieces of magician paraphernalia in the chest: flash smoke; fixed dice; a tall black hat; and an old book of magic tricks entitled A Master's Magic.

'This guy took his hobby seriously,' said Watch, picking up the hand-sized book and leafing through it. The pages were yellowed and torn, and covered with numerous handwritten notes and diagrams. Watch slipped the book in his back pocket and the moment he did so the light in the chest dimmed slightly.

'Where is that glow coming from?' Cindy asked.

'I don't know,' Adam said, staring into the chest.

'I don't know where it is coming from either,' Bryce said. 'But I know it suddenly appeared the last time we heard the cry.'

'That is true,' Watch said. 'It's almost as if whoever made the cry made it to alert us to the chest.'

'Are you saying the ghost wanted us to find this stuff?' Sally asked.

'What ghost is that?' Cindy asked her.

'Shut up,' Sally said.

'It is likely there is a connection to what we have seen and this magician's chest,' Watch said, still searching the chest with both hands. They heard a loud creak and Watch quickly sat back and whispered under his breath. 'There is a false bottom in this thing.'

'Let's not open it,' Sally said.

Bryce knelt beside the chest. 'We have to see where it leads to.' He began to remove the stuff from the chest so that they could open up the false bottom all the way. But Watch stopped him.

'I am as curious as you are, Bryce,' Watch said. 'But Sally may be right. We have to remember how many people have disappeared in this house. It might be better to stop while we're ahead of the game.'

Bryce smiled faintly. 'When have you ever left a mystery unsolved, Watch?'

Watch showed a rare smile. 'You're right.'

They pulled open the bottom of the chest.

There were stairs. They led down into darkness.

The glow inside the chest had ceased. Adam half expected to hear the cry again, from down there, but there was only silence. They all looked at each other. The question was always the same. Should they stop where they were or go on. This decision was made in silence. Slowly, one by one, they stepped inside the chest and started down the steps.

Adam led the way, Sally took up the rear. Both constantly panned left and right with their flashlights, but for a couple of minutes they could see nothing except the stairs. Then they heard a loud bang from overhead and they all stared at each other in horror.

'The trapdoor at the bottom of the chest!' Sally gasped.

They hurried back up the stairs and ran into a wooden wall. The trapdoor was shut and it would not open, no matter how hard they banged on it.

'Well that's just great!' Sally complained. 'We're trapped in here like all the other losers who never escaped this house. I told you guys that—'

'Stop,' Adam said before she could get started. 'Every time we go to do anything you tell us not to do it. If we listened to you we would never leave our homes. For now, we can't get this door open so we may as well explore further.' Adam looked at everyone. 'Agreed?'

'This may be the only way in,' Watch said. 'And the only way out. One of us might want to remain here and guard the door.'

'I'm not staying here all by myself,' Cindy said.

None of them wanted to stay, not even in pairs. They decided to continue down the stairs. After four minutes of descending, they came to a dusty wooden floor. Walls had finally appeared; these, too, were covered with a fine layer of dirt, but otherwise they were featureless. The walls enclosed a rather large auditorium. Yet the stairs came to a halt beside several open doorways.

'Which one should we take?' Adam said aloud.

'We could split up,' Bryce suggested.

'Yeah, right,' Sally muttered.

Watch pointed to a doorway at the far end of the huge room. 'Why don't we take that door. It's the largest.'

'I'm sure those who went before us chose it as well,' Sally grumbled.

'When was the last time someone disappeared in the Evil House?' Adam asked.

Watch and Bryce thought for a moment.

'I think it was a couple of Halloweens ago,' Bryce said finally.

'Yeah,' Watch agreed. 'It was Teddy Fender. He went trick or treating here. He was dressed up as a cowboy.'

'That's interesting,' Adam said. 'Did all the disappearances happen at Halloween?'

Watch and Bryce considered again.

'It's funny but I can't remember anyone disappearing around this house except at Halloween,' Watch said. 'I never thought of that before.'

'It is possible the house is only dangerous at Halloween,' Bryce said.

'That makes me feel a whole lot better,' Sally said.

Adam nodded and gestured with his flashlight towards the doorway Watch had pointed out.

'Let's see where it leads,' he said as he led them forward.

They entered a featureless passageway that went for a long way. They walked a full ten minutes and noticed no change in their surroundings. Except the dust on the wall disappeared and the temperature increased slightly.

'I'm getting thirsty,' Sally said as they plodded along in the dark.

'So am I,' Bryce said. 'I'm real thirsty and I wasn't the least bit thirsty before we entered the house. How do the rest of you feel?'

'I feel fine,' Watch said.

'Me too,' Cindy said, still carrying her fake magic wand.

Adam put his hand to his head. 'I feel slightly dizzy, but not thirsty.'

'When did you start to feel dizzy?' Watch asked.

'The moment we got down here,' Adam said.

'Curious,' Watch said, and for a moment he sounded like the real Sherlock Holmes. He took out his pipe and lit it and began to puff on it again. Only now he seemed to be inhaling because he coughed as they walked. But the rest of them were too concerned about their situation to pay much attention.

After approximately another ten minutes of walking they noticed a faint red glow up ahead. Another five minutes of walking after that and they heard vague human sounds. To their surprise it sounded as though something like a festival lay up ahead. Walking faster, they could hear people laughing and carrying on. The sound brightened everyone's mood. Almost everyone's.

'This place can't be too bad if people are laughing,' Cindy said.

But Sally remained pessimistic. 'You have to ask yourself what they're laughing at,' she said.

Eventually the passageway ended and they emerged into what looked like a deserted country lot where a century-old carnival had been erected. But they could see no sky and nothing beyond the carnival which was lit entirely by lanterns and burning torches. A huge banner stretched across the dirt entrance. It read:

MARVIN'S MAGNIFICENT MADNESS

Five

They entered the carnival and were immediately swept up in its madness. All around them were strange Halloween characters manning different exotic booths and rides. Why, the carnival's Ferris Wheel was driven by a small herd of horses that constantly circled the ride. The torches and lanterns sparked all around them. Clearly there was no electricity in Marvin's madness.

'What is this place?' Cindy gushed.

'We must be somewhere deep under Spooksville,' Sally said.

'I don't think so,' Watch said.

'What do you mean?' Adam asked. 'Of course we're under the city.'

Watch studied each of them, then looked around at the different characters yelling and cheering at their respective rides and booths.

41

'Try taking off your costumes,' Watch said finally.

'Why should we do that?' Sally asked. 'With them on we fit in here perfectly.'

'That is exactly what I mean,' Watch said. 'And that is exactly why I want you to try to take them off.'

Adam tried to pull off his sheet but found it would not come over his head. Frustrated he tried to tear it off. It was, after all, only an old sheet. But he found he could not be free of his costume. Glancing around at his friends through the two holes in his sheet, he saw they were having the same problem. Expressions of panic blossomed on all of them.

'What's wrong with me?' Cindy cried. 'I can't even put down my magic wand.'

'I can't get my cape off my back,' Bryce said.

'And I have been unable to set down my pipe ever since we ventured beneath the Evil House,' Watch said. 'I suspected that this would be the case, although I can't tell you why.'

'But what is happening?' Adam asked. 'What kind of place is this?'

'I think we have stumbled into another dimension,' Watch said seriously. 'A dimension of magic and mischief. We have to explore further, but I suspect that all the people who live in this place came here dressed in their Halloween costumes.'

Cindy trembled. 'What do you mean?'

'We will see,' Watch said, puffing on his pipe and gesturing towards a nearby fun house. A green strong-man stood outside, and waved them over. He wore black shorts and black boots and nothing else, except for masses of red lipstick. With his bulging muscles he looked like an Olympic weight-lifter that had forgotten to put down the bar.

'Come my laddies and ladies,' he said. 'Leave your fears and reason at the door. Enter a place of horror and laughter. Come, don't be afraid. All you can lose are your lives and your souls.' And with that the green strong-man let out a hearty laugh. Watch walked right up to him, all the while blowing pipe smoke.

'May I ask you a few questions?' Watch said.

The green man eyed him suspiciously. 'Are you a newcomer?'

Watch nodded. 'Yes. My friends and I are all newcomers. We're just finding our way around so pardon us if we seem naive.'

The man suddenly grabbed Watch's arm. Deep inside the fun house someone screamed in pain. The sound seemed to invigorate the green man.

'Just come in my here fun house and all your questions will be answered.'

Watch tried to shake free but was unable to. Bryce came up quickly and pushed the strong-man aside, who in turn glared at him bitterly.

'A vampire, huh?' the green strong-man said. 'We've had your kind before. We know how to deal with you. You won't last long.'

Bryce turned to Watch. 'What is he talking about?'

'Give me a minute,' Watch said, turning back to the green man. 'We don't want any trouble, sir. I would just like to know how long you have been here?'

The man frowned. 'What do you mean? I've always been here. Where else would I have been?'

'Do you mean you have always run this fun house?' Watch asked. 'Don't you remember doing anything else?'

Again the man frowned and scratched his big head. For a moment he genuinely seemed to strain to remember. But then a look of anger returned to his face.

'I have the best fun house in this here carnival,' he said. 'Don't you forget that if you want to get along here.'

Watch tried one last time. 'Were you ever a newcomer here, Sir?'

But the man was too annoyed. 'You newcomers are all the same. You are rude and ungrateful. I offer you my fun house and you insult me. You shouldn't even be allowed to enjoy the carnival. I will speak to the Master about you guys. You will pay for your insolence.'

'Show us the exit and we'll be happy to be on our way,' Sally said.

Watch held up his hand. 'We are sorry if we bothered you fine sir. It was not our intention. I pray you have a fine evening.'

The man grunted and turned away. Watch gestured for the others to follow him. 'We will get nothing out of him,' he said as they walked towards a booth that was half-covered in a cloud of smoke or steam. Above the booth was a crude sign that read:

FORTUNE-TELLER

Through the haze burned different coloured torches, some red, some green. Even more remarkable was the creature that oversaw the place. Adam had never seen a two-headed woman before. One head was

45

blonde, the other was red, although their faces were otherwise carbon copies of each other. Both wore heavy make-up. The red head was drinking a cup of coffee while the other sang to herself. The blonde head saw them first and waved them over. Except for Watch, they approached reluctantly.

'My dear ladies,' Watch said with a slight English accent. 'We are newcomers here and we have come to have our fortunes read.'

The blonde head – the one on the right – smiled, while the red head set down her cup of coffee and frowned. For Adam it was a bit disconcerting to have such opposing expressions coming from the same body. But Watch puffed on his pipe and leaned on the counter and offered his right hand to be read.

'You have come to the right place,' the blonde said.

'If you want to know what disasters await you,' the red head said.

The blonde waved her right hand. 'Ignore her. She sees disasters in everybody's futures.'

'In this place there is nothing else for us to see,' the red head said.

'What are your names?' Sally asked. From her expression, she did not look as if she had made up

her mind yet whether to feel disgusted, compass-
ionate, or just plain grossed out. The blonde smiled
at her question, however, while the red head glared
in Sally's direction.

'I am Betty,' the blonde said. 'This is Barb.'

'I can speak for myself,' Barb said.

'That you can,' Betty replied. 'But seldom with a
polite tone.'

'And who taught you your manners?' Barb asked
Betty.

'Certainly not you, Miss Sour Puss,' Betty replied.

'Miss Sour Puss?' Barb exclaimed. 'I have the
same face as you and you know it. Only my face is
far more cultured because my brain is not so
empty.'

'Your brain is the same as mine,' Betty said. 'Only
it's filled with all kinds of unhappy thoughts.' Betty
stroked her blonde hair with her right arm. Adam
assumed that Barb controlled the left arm. Betty
added, 'And my curls of gold are much more
becoming for a carnival.'

'Your curls of gold were sprayed on not two hours
ago,' Barb said.

Betty was offended. 'How dare you say that in
front of our guests!'

47

'It's true! You bleach and dye your hair every night!'

'I do not!' Betty snapped.

'You do too!'

Watch held up his free hand and continued to speak in his English accent. The rest of them had to wonder where it was coming from.

'Ladies!' he said. 'You're both adorable. Why argue who is more so? Especially when I, an English gentleman of some renown, am here to have my palm read.'

Once more Watch offered his right palm to be examined. They took it in both hands, or else they *both* took it. Betty and Barb stared at it intently. But while Betty – with her right hand – traced the lines on Watch's hand lovingly, Barb squinted and shook the hand.

'I see a bright figure,' Betty said. 'You will solve many great mysteries.'

'But they will be mysteries of murder,' Barb said. 'Death will stalk your every step.'

'You will gain fame and respect,' Betty said. 'People will come to you when they are lost and confused.'

'They will come to you in the middle of the night

and you will have no peace,' Barb said.

'You will be esteemed by your colleagues,' Betty said.

'Only to your face,' Barb said. 'Behind your back they will curse your success.'

Sally turned to the others. 'Who are they talking about?'

'Watch?' Cindy said, puzzled.

'No,' Adam said, beginning to understand. 'They are talking about Sherlock Holmes.'

'His costume has fooled them?' Bryce asked.

Adam cautioned them to be patient. 'There is more to it than that,' he said.

Watch smiled and took back his palm and puffed on his pipe.

'Thank you for your reading,' he said in his constantly improving English accent. 'It sounds like there are interesting days ahead. Now may I ask you two wonderful ladies a few questions about your futures? And your pasts?'

Betty looked pleased at the attention.

Yet Barb cast Watch a wary glance.

'Why certainly,' Betty gushed.

'What do you want to know?' Barb asked in a cold voice.

Watch leaned forward and spoke more to Betty than Barb.

'Where were you before you came to be here?' he asked softly.

Betty stiffened. 'We have always been here. Isn't that right, Barb?'

Barb stared at Watch intensely. But she was no longer scowling.

'You are new here, aren't you?' she said. 'Yes, I see that now. You are not a true part of our carnival.'

Betty shook her right hand anxiously. 'There is only our carnival. There is nothing else. Do not say these things, Barb. You know it is not permitted.'

But Barb waved her away. 'Be silent. I say what I wish.' Then she turned back to Watch, and scanned the rest of them as well. 'Where are you from?'

Watch caught her eye, 'We are all from Spooksville. But you might remember the name Springville. That is the town's proper name.' Watch again leaned forward and said, 'Springville, Barb. Springville. You remember it, don't you?'

A faraway look came over Barb's expression. Yet Betty changed from anxious to horrified. She tried to turn away from Watch, using the strength of her right side. But Barb reached out with her left hand

50

and grabbed one of the wooden poles that supported the booth. Betty fought her for a moment but then gave in and broke into sobs. But Barb was impatient with her twin's grief.

'Be silent, sister,' Barb said. 'I will speak to this man and I care not what the Master does to me.'

Betty wept in her right hand. 'What he does to you he also does to me. If you love me, please tell these people to go away.'

Barb stroked Betty's fake blonde curls with her left hand.

'I love you, sister,' she said in a softer tone. 'But the truth does not vanish simply because we pretend it doesn't exist.' Barb turned back to Watch. 'Yes, I remember Springville. When I was a young woman, before the carnival began. I was there. My name was Barbara Betty Blue and I was one of the most beautiful girls in the town.'

'I doubt you would be very popular nowadays,' Sally muttered.

'That was mean,' Cindy snapped at her.

Sally only lowered her head. But Barb had heard her, and now spoke to her instead of Watch. There was a note of sorrow in Barb's voice, as well as contempt.

51

'I see how you are dressed tonight,' Barb said. 'As a monster of the night. How long do you think you will be popular in this place? I may be hideous to you, but at least I have never hurt anyone.'

Sally looked up. 'I have never hurt anyone in my life.'

Barb gave Sally a cold smile. 'We will see if you can keep that up.'

But Watch wanted to keep things on track.

'Was your last memory of Springville Halloween night?' he asked Barb. It was no longer possible to communicate with Betty. She had buried her face in her right hand and it did not look as if she would soon be coming up for air. Barb nodded in response to Watch's question. Or Sherlock Holmes' question – Watch was acting more like the famous sleuth with each passing minute.

'Yes,' Barb said and then she sighed. 'That was many years ago but I still remember. I am probably the only one at the carnival who still does. I dressed up for Halloween and went trick or treating. I stopped at this house. It seemed just like any other house. But it was not and . . . and I ended up here.' She lowered her head and a solitary tear ran down her heavily made-up face. 'And I have never left this place and I never will.' She raised her head and sniffed. 'And I am sorry to say neither will any of you.'

Watch paused. 'What did you dress up as for that Halloween?'

Barb snorted softly and glanced over at Betty who was still sobbing.

'I am sure a man as experienced in mysteries as yourself can guess,' she replied.

Watch nodded solemnly and puffed on his pipe.

'Thank you for your time, Barb,' he said before turning away and signalling for the rest of them to follow. They gathered around Watch anxiously, but Adam had to wonder if it was Watch they were still dealing with. His whole manner had changed. He was not a kid any more, and he really was inhaling his pipe smoke.

'What was that all about?' Sally demanded.

Watch glanced at her. 'Are you still thirsty?' he asked.

'Yeah,' Sally growled. 'What does that have to do with anything?'

'Are you thirsty?' Watch asked Bryce.

Bryce nodded. 'I feel like I am dying of thirst.'

'There is a soda pop booth back there,' Watch said and pointed. 'Why don't you two go and get a drink?

I'm sure at this carnival everything is on the house.'

Sally glanced at the soda booth. 'I don't trust what they have to serve.'

Bryce also fidgeted. 'I was never a big soda drinker.'

'Is that really the problem you guys?' Watch asked.

Sally was irritated. 'If you have something to say, say it. What was Miss Two Head talking about back there?'

Watch took a moment to reply. 'Our destiny,' he said quietly.

Sally was impatient. 'Our destiny? Are you talking about their fortune-telling skills? Why my goldfish is better at reading palms than those two.'

'No,' Adam interrupted, understanding at last. He no longer felt simply light-headed but light all over. He could see that the feeling was merely a symptom of a much bigger transformation that was going on in his body. He could not take off his costume because now it was part of him. And soon the body he wore beneath the sheet would be the costume, and then that would disappear altogether. Sherlock Holmes was shrewd at solving mysteries but Adam was no slouch himself. He had eyes and ears of his won.

For the time being.

Adam turned to Sally. 'What Watch means is that we are becoming like Barb.'

Sally was stunned speechless. But Cindy was still confused.

'Are we all going to grow two heads?' Cindy asked.

'No,' Watch said gravely, in an English accent. 'We are becoming the characters we chose to be tonight. I am turning into a master sleuth, Adam is turning invisible. I bet Cindy is developing magical fairy powers without realising it.' He turned last to Bryce and Sally, who both took a step back from the group. Watch asked again, 'Are you both thirsty?'

Bryce didn't answer. Sally nodded weakly.

'Yes,' she said. 'But I still don't know why.'

'Yes you do,' Watch said. 'You just choose not to know.'

Adam nodded sadly. 'I am turning into a ghost and you guys are turning into vampires.'

Sally lowered her head and wept. Cindy tried to comfort her by patting her on the shoulder. 'Are you scared?' Cindy asked gently.

Sally looked up at her, and there was a strange eagerness in her eyes. 'No,' Sally said. 'I just want some blood.' She patted Cindy's hand and then squeezed it. Gently perhaps, or maybe hard. Sally added, 'I want it real bad.'

Cindy snapped back her hand and said it for all of them.

'Oh no,' Cindy groaned.

Six

A few moments later someone started to ring a loud bell and all the different characters at the various booths and rides dropped what they were doing and walked towards the rear of the carnival. A huge tent was erected there and the group stared in wonder at the sudden migration. They weren't sure what to do, until a mean-looking cowboy with five days' beard came by with his gun drawn. He pointed it at them.

'I hear you all is the newcomers,' he said.

'That is right, sir,' Watch said, puffing on his pipe. 'And what can we do for you this fine evening?'

The cowboy – he looked like he had been dug up from under a tumbleweed – spat out a wad of chewing tobacco and pushed his six-shooter under Watch's chin.

'It's not impressed by any fancy talk,' he said. 'You

get yourself and your pals to the magic show and you do it right now. Understand me?'

'Who's at the magic show?' Sally asked in a mocking tone. 'Marvin the Magnificent?'

The dirty cowboy didn't like her attitude. He cocked his silver revolver and pointed the barrel between her eyebrows.

'You makin' fun of the Master?' he demanded.

Sally snorted. 'He ain't my Master, you old dust cloud.'

Watch immediately stepped in front of Sally. For it looked as if the cowboy was about to put a lead bullet in her head. Watch held up a hand.

'We were just on our way to the magic show,' Watch said in his English accent. 'Thank you, kind sir, for reminding us that we are late.'

The cowboy lowered his pistol and again spat on the ground. He growled in Sally's direction and spoke to Watch.

'You keep that young thing under control, you hear me?' he said. 'Or else there will be another funeral around here soon. Ain't no one speak against the Master and live long. Not while Wild Bill walks the town.'

The cowboy sauntered off.

'Was that the real Wild Bill?' Cindy asked. 'He didn't have very good manners.'

'Of course it wasn't the real one,' Watch said. 'That guy – he was probably a kid before he came here – just came here as the character of Wild Bill. But as he stayed here he became him, or at least he thinks he became him. That's what I'm trying to tell you guys.'

Adam squeezed his arm. At least he could still feel it. On the other hand, he had to wonder if the others could still feel him. But he was afraid to experiment, afraid to find out how quickly he was changing.

'We'd better get to the show,' Adam said, 'before anyone else tries to kill us. And Sally, you're going to have to watch your mouth in this place. We're still not sure what we're dealing with here.'

They began to walk in the direction of the huge tent. Already the rest of the carnival grounds were empty. Bryce raised an interesting point as they walked.

'I find it more than a coincidence that Marvin the Magnificent is the boss around here,' Bryce said. 'And we just happened to enter this realm from his bedroom. Is it possible he has somehow created this dimension?'

Watch nodded. 'Elementary, my dear Bryce. I have been thinking the same thing.'

Bryce paused. 'Are you going to be talking like Sherlock Holmes the rest of the night?' he asked Watch.

Watch was apologetic. 'I can't help it, my dear Watson. I mean, I am sorry Bryce. But back to your keen observation. I believe as you do that Marvin, must be at the basis of this strange carnival.'

'But that's impossible,' Cindy said. 'Marvin lived over a hundred years ago.'

Watch glanced in the direction of the tent. 'How many people have we heard about who have disappeared in and around the Evil House?' he asked. 'Maybe four or five in our lifetime. Yet there must be over a hundred people here. I think Marvin has been collecting them for at least a hundred years.'

'Collecting them?' Cindy asked. 'She didn't like the sound of that.

'Are you saying we've been collected?' Adam asked.

Watch puffed on his pipe and frowned. 'The night is still young. Let us not lose hope. Come, we have been ordered to the magic show and we will go.'

The interior of the tent was packed. Everyone was

60

a freak: ghouls and zombies; pirates and mermaids. The seats were set in a semicircle round a small wooden stage that had been covered with white paper. They had hardly made themselves comfortable when there was a flash of smoke and the torches dimmed. They brightened a moment later and, lo and behold, Marvin the Magnificent was standing there in a black and white tux.

Unlike the other characters, he was still a boy.

Indeed, he still looked like his old photo.

Watch leaned over and whispered these facts to the rest of them.

'But what does it mean?' Cindy said.

'That Marvin is the key,' Watch said confidently. 'Everything revolves around him in this place, and yet he has not grown old.'

'Everybody grows old,' Sally said.

'Maybe his magic keeps him young,' Bryce suggested.

Watch was thoughtful. 'Maybe it is something else.'

Marvin spoke in a loud voice. Although he still sounded young, there was a strange power in his tone. He was the *Master* and he knew it.

'Welcome to another evening of magic and

mystery,' he said. 'Tonight is a great night for all of us, the chosen ones, the beautiful ones, the happy ones. For tonight we will see feats that defy all reason. Miracles that cannot be explained.' Martin gestured with his hand and bowed slightly. 'Thank you all for coming.'

The applause was quick and loud, out of all proportion to anything Marvin had said or done. But then Adam saw Wild Bill wandering the sidelines with Mr Green Strong-Man. They were Marvin's muscle, Adam realised. If the people didn't cheer loudly and with enthusiasm something probably happened to them.

That *something* was made clear a moment later.

'Now before I begin I need a volunteer from the audience,' Marvin said. The crowd fell instantly silent as he scanned the seats. Marvin smiled as he searched, and it was a chilling smile – innocence mixed with ruthlessness. He added in a cold voice, 'Come, doesn't anyone want to take a chance and be a part of history?' Marvin paused and pointed to a Viking warrior who was seated in the third row. 'You, sir. You come up here now.'

The warrior paled. Although a thick sword rested on his lap, it fell from his grasp as he climbed to his wobbly feet. Apparently being a *volunteer* in one of Marvin's magic tricks was an unhealthy occupation. The warrior trembled as he spoke.

'But Master,' he said, 'I have served you faithfully for many long years.' He lowered his big hairy head and began to sob quietly. 'I don't understand why you have chosen me.'

But Marvin giggled. 'Don't be afraid, Cleytor. This is one of my favourite tricks and you know how good I am.' Marvin addressed the whole audience. 'I am good, am I not?'

The crowd cheered enthusiastically. Wild Bill came up behind Cleytor and put a gun to the warrior's head.

'You get on up on that there stage this second,' Wild Bill said. 'And stop that crying. It makes me want to spit.'

Cleytor slowly walked towards the stage – Wild Bill spat anyway – while the crowd roared its approval. Or maybe they roared with relief that none of them had been chosen. Adam saw Barb – and Betty – at the front and wondered what they thought of this magic show.

Cleytor finally reached the stage. He tried to dry his face but was having trouble. Marvin patted him gently on the back and his assistant – a gorilla – wheeled out a long black box. Marvin wanted Cleytor to get in it but the Viking warrior burst into heart-wrenching sobs.

'Please don't put me in the box!' he wept. 'I don't want to go in the box!'

Marvin giggled and drew out a large saw from inside his tux.

'Don't worry!' he said. 'I'll get you out of that box right away!'

The crowd roared once again.

'This is sick,' Sally whispered. 'He's going to kill that poor man.'

'Don't interfere or he will kill you,' Watch warned.

'But we can't just sit here and let him do it,' Adam protested.

Watch was firm. 'We can and we will. Now do what everyone else is doing. Cheer when you're supposed to.'

Wild Bill and Mr Green Strong-man came on to the stage and forced weeping Cleytor into the box. It was not big enough for the warrior but no matter. His head stuck out one end, his legs the other. He continued to struggle but it was hopeless. The gorilla – it looked like a real one – threw some latches on top of the black box and the warrior was locked inside. Marvin half danced across the stage, showing everyone how shiny and sharp his saw was.

'Now you might all be wondering what I am going to do with this saw!' Marvin said to the cheering crowd. 'You might be wondering if I am going to saw this poor man in half! Well wonder no more! This man is already two big pieces of meat!'

'We've got to stop him,' Cindy moaned, moving to get up.

Watch put a hand on her leg. 'We've got to get more information before we do anything. Now sit still and don't interfere.

Wearing a fiendish grin, Marvin stepped towards the black box and began to saw down the centre of it. Cleytor howled in pain, although it was doubtful the blade of the saw had reached him yet. For the gang the torture was unbearable because they had no doubt that this was no magic act at all, but a tent of torture. Adam fidgeted in his seat, unable to watch.

Marvin suddenly paused and glanced back at the audience.

'Should I use my magic?' he asked the crowd. 'Or should I save it for a rainy day?'

'A rainy day!' the crowd shouted back.

'Use your magic!' Cleytor cried, alone. No, not quite alone. The gang – including Watch, who wasn't listening to his own advice – yelled out, 'Use your magic' along with Cleytor. The trouble was that their shout drew Marvin's attention. The kid magician paused and looked over at them.

'Is that the newcomers?' he asked aloud.

Watch stood. 'We just arrived tonight, yes. May we be of some service to you?'

Marvin lost his smile. 'On my next trick. Sit down and behave.'

Watch sat back down. Sally hissed at him.

'You didn't have to volunteer us,' she said.

'That may have been a mistake,' Watch admitted.

Marvin returned to his dirty work. The edges of the box splintered, the saw ploughed deeper. Cleytor began to scream and then to choke. The blade finally began to slow; even Marvin could not make it work faster. The steel had found its victim.

A flood of black fluid began to drip from the bottom of the box.

Cindy buried her face in her hands. 'Somebody help us!' she cried.

Sally and Bryce licked their lips.

'Looks like nice warm blood,' Sally said.

'And there's plenty of it,' Bryce agreed.

Watch and Adam looked over at them and felt very uneasy.

Again Marvin appealed to the crowd. 'Should I cut him in two or use my magic?' he shouted.

The crowd knew they had to give the thumbs down.

'Cut him in two!' they yelled.

Watch suddenly stood up. 'Use your lousy magic!' he shouted.

The tent fell dead silent. Adam leaned over and spoke to his friend.

'You just told us not to draw attention to ourselves,' Adam said. 'Now look what you've done.'

'I wouldn't mind licking that blood off the floor,' Sally whispered to Bryce.

'Maybe we can find a couple of straws,' Bryce agreed.

'Would you two stop talking like that,' Cindy snapped at them. 'You're making me sick.'

Watch spoke to Adam. 'I just remembered how this trick works.' Then he stopped suddenly and thought a moment. 'No. That was another trick. Never mind.' He went to sit down. Unfortunately he now had Marvin's full attention.

'Remain standing!' Marvin ordered as he stepped away from the black box with his bloody saw. Cleytor seemed to have gone into shock. He was no longer crying or making any sound, except for maybe a faint choking noise. Marvin walked towards Watch and asked in a demanding voice, 'What do you mean my magic is lousy?'

Watch swallowed. 'What I meant was that you lack the power to even saw my friend in half.'

'Which friend is he talking about?' Sally hissed to the others.

Watch gestured to Adam, who sat beneath his white sheet.

'Instead of cutting up that crybaby warrior,' Watch said. 'Let us see you cut up a real man, like my friend Adam!'

Adam had to wonder if he had heard his friend aright.

'Why are you volunteering to have me murdered?' he whispered to Watch.

'Just go along and don't worry,' Watch said quietly.

'Don't worry?' Adam gasped. 'That's a real saw he has there!'

'It does look real,' Watch agreed.

Sally turned to Bryce. 'I don't think I could drink Adam's blood,' she said.

Bryce rubbed his dry throat. 'I would rather not have to, but I am awfully thirsty.'

'Stop it!' Cindy yelled at everyone.

Marvin was interested. 'Send your friend down. We will see how tough his hide is.'

'Release Cleytor and Adam will be more than happy to climb into your black box,' Watch said.

'Agreed!' Marvin shouted back.

Adam jumped up. 'I would not be more than happy!' he shouted at Watch. 'What kind of Sherlock Holmes are you anyway? You're supposed to solve mysteries! You're not supposed to get people slaughtered!'

Watch puffed on his pipe. 'Elementary, my dear Adam.'

'What the heck does that mean?' Adam demanded.

Watch paused. 'Just trust me.'

The gorilla let Cleytor out of the black box and led him off to see the local nurse. Apparently the carnival had a couple of them. Wild Bill and Mr Green Strong-Man came into the stands for Adam, but Adam had too much pride to be dragged to his death. Trying to look calm – under his white sheet – he stepped on to the stage. Marvin waited for him with his fiendish grin and his bloody saw.

'Do you have any final words?' he asked.

'I just hope you're a great magician,' Adam said.

Marvin leaned closer and Adam saw just how young he was, even younger than himself. 'I am magnificent,' Marvin confided. 'But only when I am in the mood.' He paused. 'Get in the box.'

Adam climbed into the box and was locked in. His head stuck out one end but not his feet. He was not as tall as the Viking Warrior. The crowd fell silent as Marvin approached and put the blade to the already splintered wood.

'Are you afraid?' Marvin asked Adam.

'I suppose you could say that,' Adam gulped.

'You should be.' Then Marvin shouted to the audience. 'Mercy or pain?'

'Pain!' they shouted back in unison.

'I could maybe drink Adam's blood if my eyes were closed,' Sally muttered, panting.

'I think I could drink it if it was mixed with apple juice or something,' Bryce said.

Cindy cringed. 'You two are monsters!'

Sally nodded and licked her lips. 'Getting there I'm sorry to say.'

Marvin began to saw. Adam could see the blade moving swiftly through the already cut up wood and he began to panic. He forced a smile under his sheet.

'I really would love to see some of your magic,' he told Marvin.

'I'm not in the mood,' Marvin said and kept sawing.

Up in the stands Cindy wept and pointed an accusing finger at Watch.

'How could you do this to your friend?' she demanded.

Watch continued to puff on his pipe. 'A calculated risk, my dear.'

'I am not your dear!' Cindy shouted.

Watch was taken aback. 'It's just a manner of speaking.'

Down on the stage Adam squirmed inside the box.

'I thought the posters in your bedroom were cool,' he told Marvin.

Marvin paused. 'You really liked them?'

Adam gushed. 'Oh yes! They were wonderful!'

Marvin shrugged. 'I never much cared for them.'

Marvin returned to sawing. The blade kept coming closer and closer.

Adam wanted to scream. Maybe he did start screaming, he wasn't sure.

Yet the pain never came. The blade never cut into his flesh.

Magic did happen. Or maybe it was a miracle.

When the saw did reach where his body was trapped in the box, it began to *pass right through him*. Adam was so astounded that he almost wept with relief. But when Marvin realised what was happening he threw his saw aside in disgust and spoke to Adam with bitterness.

'You have changed fast for a newcomer,' he said. 'Your transformation to a ghost is almost complete. I should have foreseen that before accepting your friend's challenge. You have embarrassed me in front of my people.'

Adam smiled under his sheet, which was beginning to feel more like a white cloud hugging his body. 'I'm sorry, really,' he said. 'Can I get out of the box now?'

Marvin gestured to his gorilla assistant to remove the latches. The audience continued to sit silently, but watched closely. They had probably never seen Marvin's designs foiled before. Up in the stands Cindy and the others were looking at Watch with newfound respect, even though Sally and Bryce also appeared disappointed. They both knew they were going to have to drink some blood soon or else go stark raving mad.

Suddenly Marvin forced a laugh and shouted to the crowd.

'I just wanted to scare the newcomers a bit!' he said. 'But let's not let them think we are inhospitable. This is after all a carnival. Tonight they will dine with me in comfort at my mansion. Agreed?'

The crowd shouted its agreement. Yet mixed in with the noise were sounds of surprise. Their Master had been out-foxed and they knew it. In the stands, Sally turned to Bryce.

'We can't hope that anyone dies at Marvin's house tonight,' she said. 'It would be bad luck to make such a wish.'

'You're right,' Bryce agreed.

Sally swallowed in her horribly dry throat and looked at all the nice healthy people and healthy monsters – with healthy blood in their veins – all around her. Her thirst was now a constant ache.

'But maybe somebody will die anyway,' she said with a note of hope in her voice.

Seven

They travelled to Marvin's mansion in a horse-drawn carriage. But Marvin did not sit inside with them. Apparently he liked to be up front with the coachman, or else he was still mad at them. Yet there was one companion from the gang that he didn't mind talking to. As they left the carnival tent – with the crowd still muttering about the Master's embarrassment – Marvin seemed to take a fancy to Cindy. He asked her to ride up front with him. Watch encouraged her to do what he asked.

'Find out what you can about him,' Watch told her.

Now they were travelling through what could best be described as a twilight zone. The stage coach had exited the rear of the carnival ground through an unguarded gate, on to a dark road that seemed to lead only to more darkness. They could see Cindy out-side the window of the carriage, sitting with Marvin, but the two did not seem to be talking. They were the only thing they could see, besides the coachman, who wore a huge white hat that shielded his face. The horizon seemed much closer than usual – a grey wall of nothing. It was Watch's opinion that the people of the carnival did not leave the grounds because there was nowhere else to go.

'But that can't be true,' Adam said, sitting in the cramped interior of the carriage with his friends. Of course it wasn't really cramped for Adam because solid objects had a way of ignoring the borders of his body now. Not that he actually let anything go through his body. The idea still made him queasy. Adam added, 'We must be going somewhere.'

'Yes and no,' Watch said. 'I believe everything in this dimension is a prop of sorts. It only exists because Marvin wished it to exist.'

'You think that he is that great a magician?' Sally asked.

Watch considered. 'He does not seem like such a powerful personality that he should have special powers. But it is possible he somehow tapped into someone else's source of power.'

'What does that mean?' Sally asked.

'That he had help,' Bryce said. He added, 'Hey, Watch, it's kind of cramped over here. Can I sit next to you?'

Watch, who was sitting with Adam, appeared uncomfortable. 'I would rather you two stayed where you were,' he said.

'You're not afraid of us, are you?' Sally asked.

'Let me ask you guys a question,' Watch said. 'Are you thinking of drinking my blood?'

'Of course not,' Sally said.

'Yeah,' Bryce said. 'It could be anyone's blood. It doesn't have to be yours.'

'But since Adam is already halfway to being a ghost,' Watch said, 'and you two are practically vampires. I am the only one riding in this carriage with warm blood flowing through my veins. For that reason I would prefer to keep my distance.'

'You wouldn't want to give us just a little taste?' Sally asked, licking her red lips. 'You could prick your finger just a tiny bit.'

'No thank you,' Watch said quickly.

'Just a drop,' Bryce said. 'It won't harm you.'

'No,' Watch said firmly.

'Coward.' Sally muttered.

77

'Doesn't the idea of drinking blood gross you out?' Adam asked.

'Actually it sounds like a wonderful idea,' Bryce said.

'How does the idea of going around and scaring little kids sound to you?' Sally asked Adam. Her friend brightened at the question.

'That sounds like fun,' Adam said, before catching himself. 'What's wrong with my mind? Hey, Watch, are you feeling any negative side effects of this transformation?'

Watch puffed away. 'I just want to get to the bottom of his mystery.'

'That figures,' Sally muttered, glancing out of the window once more. 'Hey, I don't think that Cindy is doing our case any good. She's not even flirting with Marvin yet.'

'Give her time,' Adam said.

'Why do you say that?' Sally grumbled. 'Did it only take time before she started flirting with you?'

'Oh brother,' Adam muttered.

'If Cindy isn't talking to Marvin then maybe she should come back and sit with us,' Bryce suggested.

'I don't think so,' Watch said dryly.

Sally showed her fangs. 'I wouldn't hurt her. I promise.'

'She is fine where she is,' Adam said, worried how long it would be before Sally and Bryce did hurt someone. They were looking more monstrous by the minute.

Actually Cindy was making inroads with Marvin, only slowly. When they first left the carnival, Marvin seemed too angry to speak to. But now the ride in the night air had appeared to cool him off. He finally looked over at her and smiled. The coachman rode beside them, silently, with a huge hat covering his head. The man looked a little funny but Cindy was not sure why.

'Are you having fun here?' Marvin asked.

Cindy knew she had to move carefully.

'We just got here,' she said. 'It seems like an exciting place.'

'Don't talk abut we,' Marvin said. 'Talk about you.'

'All right,' Cindy said diplomatically. 'I'll talk about me if you talk about you.'

'That sounds fair,' Marvin said, with a trace of hesitation. He glanced up and down at her fairy princess costume, and at her glittering wand. Even in

79

the poor light the wand seemed to shimmer with a magical glow. He added, 'What character did you dress up as for Halloween?'

She sensed the question was important to him, and she was finally beginning to understand why that was the case. Cindy was no dummy when it came to putting pieces of a mystery together. What they were dressed as when they left their homes is what they were now. She laughed softly before answering to make him uneasy.

'I dressed up as the princess of all the fairies,' she said.

Marvin blinked. 'That's exciting.'

She continued to giggle. 'I know. I can't wait to use my magic wand.' She raised her wand to point at something off the road. But Marvin quickly grabbed it and made her lower it.

'That wouldn't be a good idea,' he said.

She quietened. 'Are you afraid of something?'

He waved his hand. 'I am the Master here. Nothing can harm me.'

She sensed falseness in his tone.

'How long have you been here?' she asked.

He stared off into the distance, thoughtful. 'A long time, Cindy.'

'You know my name?'

'Of course.'

'How?' she asked.

He shrugged. 'Magic.'

'You like doing magic on stage, don't you?'

He paused. 'I still like it.' He didn't sound like he meant it.

'Did you really hurt that Viking warrior?'

He smiled slyly. 'What do you think?'

She decided she needed to be honest. Sometimes, even with a monster, that was the best policy. In reality she didn't trust Marvin at all. His forced politeness did not hide his cruelty.

'I don't know,' she said. 'I don't know you that well.'

He grinned, and it was the wicked grin he had shown on stage.

'I think we are going to get to know each other extremely well,' he said.

'How did you end up here?' she asked.

He acted annoyed. His mood could change quickly.

'Is it fair that I have to answer all your questions?' he said. 'You are my guest. You should answer some of mine.'

'Ask away. I have nothing to hide.'

He considered. 'What is Springville like these days?'

'Spooky. It's called Spooksville nowadays.'

'Spooksville! I love it! What goes on in town?'

Cindy frowned. 'Just about everything.'

'Is there still a witch?' he asked.

'Sure. Ann Templeton. We saw her tonight. We went trick or treating at her castle.'

He was interested. 'What did she give you?'

'Just some advice.'

'What was it?' he asked.

I understand, Cindy. You are afraid, and that is not necessarily a bad thing in this town. But remember this is Halloween night. Strange things happen this time of year. This very night you might find yourself in a very unusual place. A place where fear can kill you, and only your power can save others. Remember that, Cindy, won't you? My fairy princess.

Cindy realised with a shock that Ann Templeton had known what was going to happen to them. And had given her a special instruction to deal with the emergency.

Cindy shrugged. 'I can't remember.'

Marvin stared at her a moment. 'Are you sure?'

'Yes. It was nothing important.'

Marvin stared at her a moment longer and then smiled suddenly. To her surprise he put his arm round her shoulder. She couldn't help noticing that he kept his other hand close to her magic wand.

'You and I are going to get along fabulously,' he said.

Cindy had to bite her lip to keep from saying, *I don't think so*.

Eight

Marvin's mansion looked very much like the Evil House in shape and design, only it was larger and in better condition. What was even more strange was that they could see the ocean in the distance, in the dark. Yet there was something funny about the water. Watch squinted at it as they all climbed out of the carriage. Finally he spoke to the others who had been in the rear of the carriage with him.

'The wave pattern on the water is faint,' he said. 'Especially at this distance. But I think it keeps repeating itself.'

'But what does that mean?' Sally asked.

'That the ocean is just another prop,' Bryce said, looking around the outside of the house. 'I wonder if there are any little plump animals around here.'

'You would drink the blood of a little animal?'

Sally asked. 'That's disgusting. I will have a human being or nothing at all.'

'Who is disgusting?' Adam muttered.

Sally went to poke him in the chest but her finger seemed to momentarily go through Adam. He jumped back as if stabbed but in reality he did not seem hurt.

'Listen Mr Casper the Ghost,' Sally said. 'Just because you're turning into an immaterial ball of light that has no physical needs doesn't mean the rest of us are so lucky. I'm a vampire, I need blood. There's nothing wrong with that.'

Watch was thoughtful. 'Adam is not the first ghost we saw this evening.'

'Actually a ghost was the only creature we saw in the Evil House proper,' Bryce said. 'Do you think that's a coincidence?'

Watch puffed on his pipe. 'I don't believe in coincidences, only in clues.'

Marvin and Cindy finally climbed down from the front of the carriage. The coachman with the big hat had already taken off for the inside of the mansion. None of them had really got a good look at him beneath his costume. Marvin looked in a pleasant mood although Cindy seemed worried.

'Why don't each of you retire to your prepared rooms for an hour or so and freshen up?' he said. 'Then I will send somebody for you and we can have dinner together.'

'We would rather not be separated from each other,' Adam said.

Marvin scowled. 'Now that isn't a very polite remark, is it? You are with Marvin the Magnificent, and in his own realm. You are completely safe.'

'Do you have extra servants that you are not particularly fond of?' Sally asked.

Cindy frowned. 'Are you still hungry for blood?'

'I'm not craving a pizza, sister,' Sally grumbled.

Marvin laughed at Sally's question and gestured to his front door.

'All your needs will be taken care of in time,' he said.

It was his show, they had no choice but to go along with his charade, if that's in fact what it was. Inside the house were a number of butlers – each in proper black and white costume – who quickly led them in the direction of their rooms. They caught only a faint glimpse of the mansion along the way. Besides being huge, it was also like the Evil House in that the style of furniture was from the last century.

87

Also, there were no pictures, no mirrors. It was as if Marvin did not want to be reminded of the past, or even of himself. Watch leaned over and whispered to Cindy as they were led up a wide set of stairs.

'Did you find out anything interesting?' he asked.

'I think so,' she whispered back. 'Marvin is interested in me because I am a fairy princess with a magical wand. I also think he likes me because he is lonely in this place.'

'He could have picked better company,' Sally said. Then she added, 'Hey, Cindy, I think us girls should room together.'

'Trust me, you do not want to room with either of the vampires,' Adam said.

'That wasn't very nice,' Sally said. 'I'm not going to try to drink her blood, not much of it.'

'Did you get the sense that he wants to leave this place?' Watch asked Cindy.

She considered. 'That's an interesting question. I think that might be true. When he spoke of how long he had been here, he sounded sad.'

'Maybe there will be a fruit basket and a chalice of blood in our rooms,' Bryce said hopefully to Sally.

'I like to see where my blood comes from,' Sally said.

'What are we going to do in the next hour before dinner?' Adam asked as they reached the top of the stairs and started down a long hallway, still in the company of their various butlers. They didn't know where Marvin had run off to.

'As soon as we get to our rooms,' Watch said, 'and the butlers have left, we have to try to regroup. We have to talk and figure out a strategy.'

'Are we invited?' Sally asked.

'We are tired of being outcasts,' Bryce said.

'If you behave yourselves you are invited,' Watch said.

Each of the butlers led them into a different room. The suites were plush, with beautiful long drapes, nice carpet, big beds. But each of them had been inside no more than a few seconds when they each heard the door click locked behind them. The butlers had shut each of them in. All five of them ended up pressed against their different doors, pounding with their fists and listening for what the others might be saying.

'Can you guys hear me?' Sally called.

'I can hear you,' Bryce called back.

'We can hear each other because we're vampires,' Sally said. 'Can the others hear us?'

It did not seem that they could. Certainly Watch couldn't – he couldn't hear very well under ordinary circumstances. Alone in his room, Watch sat down on the edge of the bed and pulled out of his pocket the book of magic tricks he had found in the chest at the end of Marvin's bed: *A Master's Magic*. He recalled how the bottom of the chest had opened right after he had picked up the book. It was almost as if the book was a key that led to the secret realm. Elementary, my dear Watson, he thought. He would have to think about that clue some more. Glancing through the book, he noticed for the first time that many of the magic instructions were in secret codes, also recorded in strange characters. Almost as if they had been written in a separate time from known history, another age. Watch puffed on his pipe and finally put the book back in his pocket.

There was a knock at the door. Watch got up and stepped to it.

'Hello?' he called.

The door suddenly swung open. Wild Bill stood dirty and mean in the hallway, his gun pointed at Watch's head. He grinned as he cocked his revolver.

'I am here to take you to dinner, partner,' he said.

Watch glanced up and down the hallway. 'Where are my friends?'

'They will be joining you shortly,' Wild Bill said, and spat on the floor. 'Move along now, before I have to put a slug of lead in your fat brain.'

'My brain is not technically fat,' Watch said. 'It is just superior to yours.'

Wild Bill grabbed him by the arm and yanked him out of the room, shoving him further down the hallway. 'Get moving and quit talking. I ain't impressed by you big worded cowards. The Master's got plans for you guys.'

'I'm sure he has,' Watch muttered as he was led down another stairway. This one did not lead to the entrance or to the dining-room but to a dark place. A dungeon from which he suspected few escaped. Watch wondered just how many would be having dinner with Marvin the Magnificent tonight.

Nine

The answer to Watch's question was *one*. Cindy was still alone in her room, an hour later, when her butler came for her. And she was alone in the vast dining-room when the butler left her. There was a meal prepared on the table but it was only for two people. She immediately suspected that Marvin wanted to probe the extent of her fairy princess powers in private. She wondered about those powers herself. She had tried a few tricks alone in her room with her wand and nothing had happened. If she had magic it was taking its time showing up.

Marvin slipped into the room behind her when she wasn't looking.

'Hungry?' he asked.

His question startled her. She turned quickly.

'Where are my friends?' she asked.

He spread his hands innocently. 'I suppose they're still resting in their rooms.'

'I want to see them.'

Marvin gestured for her to sit. 'Relax, they are safe. Let us enjoy a few quiet moments together. Come, eat, you must be hungry.'

Cindy was in fact starving. She had not even had dinner before they had started trick or treating. The last time she had eaten had been lunch at school. Boy, that seemed like ages ago. What a weird day it had been so far, she thought.

Cindy sat down at the table and began to pick at her food – roast turkey and mashed potatoes, one of her favourite dinners. Marvin sat down opposite her, pleased that she was at least trying the food.

'Is it good?' he asked.

'It would be better if my friends were here to enjoy it with me,' she said.

He forced a smile. 'You don't trust me, do you?'

'Should I? The first time I see you, you're torturing an unwilling volunteer from your audience.'

He waved his hand. 'Oh that. That was nothing. Cleytor is all right. He's just a big baby. That was fake blood that poured out of the box.'

'It looked real to me.'

Marvin was thoughtful for a moment. 'Nothing is really real here.'

She noticed a trace of sorrow in his tone. 'It's all just a produce of your magic?' she asked.

He nodded and gestured around him. 'None of this would exist without me.'

'But how were you able to create it all?' she asked. 'Where did you get the power?'

He drew back as if offended by her question.

'My magic has always been very powerful,' he said.

Cindy remembered how he had quizzed her about the town witch.

'Did you know any of Ann Templeton's ancestors?' she asked.

She had scored a bullseye. He literally jumped at her question.

'I knew Madeline Templeton,' he admitted.

Cindy whistled. 'She lived a long time ago. She was one of the founding members of Spooksville – Springville. How did you know her?'

Marvin shrugged, looking guilty. 'She was just someone in town that liked me.'

'She wasn't just someone in town, Marvin. She was the town witch.' Cindy paused. Something had just occurred to her. 'Did you go trick or treating at her house at Halloween?'

Marvin was uncomfortable. 'Yes. How did you know?'

'It doesn't matter. Did she give you a treat?'

'Sure.'

'What was it?'

He shrugged again. 'Just a book on magic tricks.'

She recalled the book Watch had found in the wooden chest at the foot of Marvin's bed. It had looked very old and unusual.

'Did this book make you a better magician?' she asked.

Marvin stood suddenly, angry, and stepped away. He had his mood swings.

'I don't have to answer any of these questions!' he shouted.

Cindy stared at him in surprise. 'Why do they bother you?'

He whirled round. 'All right, I used some of the spells in Madeline Templeton's book when I got sick. I used them to make myself better. But that was the only time I used them. Otherwise, all my magic is mine and mine alone. I am a true magician, the greatest in the whole world.'

Cindy felt as if she had just been told something important.

'How sick were you?' she asked quietly.

Marvin seemed to force himself to be calm and sat back down.

'I had a chest cold and a bad fever,' he said. 'I kept coughing, I couldn't breathe. I don't know what it's like to get that sick in your time, but back then you usually died. I almost died, my parents thought I was going to. But then I opened the book Madeline gave to me and performed a few magic spells that related to healing. Then I felt better.'

'Your parents must have been relieved,' Cindy said.

Marvin shook his head. 'I didn't see them after that.'

'Why not?'

'Because I came here.'

'Here?' Cindy asked. 'You came here on purpose?'

He appeared uneasy. 'Of course. I love this place. Here I am Master. But then others started to come, slowly over the years, and I was able to control each of them, even after they changed.'

'Why do people change here?' she asked.

'It is just what happens. It is because my magic is so strong here.'

She felt as if he was giving himself more credit than he deserved.

'Why do you have to control everyone?' she asked.

'Somebody has to. Without control there would be no order. The carnival would run wild.'

'Did you set up the carnival?'

'Yes.'

'Why?' she asked.

'I like it.' He laughed. 'And I had so many characters coming here that could only fit in a carnival. I mean, where else can you put a green strong-man except in a freak show?'

'What do you want with me?' she asked.

Marvin quietened. 'What makes you think I want anything from you?'

She eyed him carefully. 'I can tell. Why don't you just tell me what you want and get it out in the open?'

He stared at her and nodded slowly. 'All right, Cindy, I will tell you the truth. As you have guessed, I have gotten somewhat bored with this place. I've been here a long time, you see. I would like to see other places, meet new people.'

'You must know that outside of your realm you can't control everybody you meet,' she said with a trace of anger. He quickly held up a hand.

'I have no intention of doing that,' he said. 'I just want to leave it all.'

'But what do you need me for? Isn't your magic strong enough to open the trapdoor that leads back up to your bedroom?'

He seemed surprised. 'You know about that?'

'Of course. It locked on us when we came down here. Can't you open it? I assumed that you could.'

Marvin looked pained. 'Well, no, I can't open it. I don't know why but my magic doesn't work on it.'

'So you are trapped here, like everyone else,' Cindy said.

'In a sense. But that's where you come in. I haven't had a fairy princess visit before. Really, no one has shown up with magical powers in the last hundred years. But here you are now, and I was thinking that you might be able to use your magic wand and put a spell on the trapdoor beneath my old bedroom and make it open. Then I could get back out in the world, maybe even go to see my parents again.'

Cindy spoke carefully. 'Marvin. You said it yourself how long you have been here. Your parents are surely dead.'

Her remarks took him back a step. He seemed to

pale, but he fought to hide any other signs of grief.

'That might be true,' he admitted. 'But even if it is, I still need to get out of here.' He paused. 'Will you help me?'

Cindy considered. 'Say I am able to help you. Will you let all the others who are trapped here go?'

Marvin sneered. 'Why would I want to do that?'

Cindy leaned towards him on the table. 'Because they are slaves here, and no one should be treated like a slave. You have to let them go.'

Marvin shook his head vigorously. 'That's impossible. I have been their Master for too many years. They have been under my command for too long. If I suddenly release them, it will be a disaster.'

'You mean you have treated them so badly over the years that if you suddenly release them they might turn against you? Isn't that what you're really saying?'

Marvin's face flushed with blood. He was suddenly furious.

'How dare you accuse me in my own house!' he yelled. 'I don't have to help them if I don't want to. We are talking about me here, Marvin the Magnificent! No one defies me! You help me get out of here, Cindy, or you will regret it! I will make you regret it!'

Cindy sat quietly and then shook her head.

'You're crazy,' she said finally. 'Worse, you are cruel. I will never help you. I don't care what you do to me.'

Marvin slowly stood and glared down at her.

'It is not what I can do to you that will hurt you,' he said wickedly. 'It is what I can do to your friends. You see, Cindy, they are not really resting in their rooms.'

Ten

The gang was in fact resting in a black dungeon. They had all been dragged there by an assortment of carnival characters. Except for a low burning torch, the place was black, hemmed in on every side with stone walls. Watch sat in one corner and puffed on his pipe while Adam sat in the other and glowed. Sally and Bryce could not stop pacing. Their thirst was killing them. Every time they stepped past Watch, they stared at him hungrily.

'If you just gave us a pint of blood each,' Sally complained to Watch. 'It wouldn't kill you.'

'Even a half pint each would be appreciated,' Bryce added.

Watch glanced up at them. 'Once you start drinking my blood you won't be able to stop. You'll drink me dry.'

Sally knelt in front of Watch. She leaned over and brushed his hair aside.

'I promise to stop drinking your blood if you start to turn blue,' she said.

Watch turned his head aside. 'You're a vampire, you won't be able to stop yourself. Better you don't start.'

'That's easy for you to say,' Bryce said. 'But this thirst is driving me crazy.' He paused and looked down at Watch. 'You know we have grown strong. We could take your blood if we wanted to.'

The threat hung in the air like a cloud of foul air. But of course that is what Marvin must have had in mind when he locked them up together. That they would eventually start to kill one another. Adam stood and gave his vampire friends an angry look.

'If you two are so strong,' he said. 'Why don't you break down the door?'

'You saw us try,' Sally said, standing and stepping away from Watch. 'It is too strong, even for us.'

'But if we had even a little blood we might have more strength,' Bryce said.

'Would you stop talking about drinking Watch's blood!' Adam shouted. But his voice came out rather high and squeaky. It had been changing all night.

Soon he would sound like the ghost that had been haunting the Evil House. He said as much to the others and Watch glanced at him.

'That ghost has been bothering me,' Watch said. 'It was the only supernatural creature in the Evil House. In fact, if you guys remember, we only started to change after we got trapped beneath the trapdoor.'

'But the ghost is above the trapdoor,' Adam said. 'I don't understand what you're saying.'

'That is exactly the point I am trying to make,' Watch said. 'The ghost in the Evil House is different to all the characters down here. Yet in a sense it led us down here. It must be connected to this place.'

'But whose ghost is it?' Sally asked.

Watch stood and gestured with his pipe. 'Elementary, my dear Sally. That is the most important question. Who is that ghost? And there are a couple of other important questions. Why was he there in the house? Why did he lead us down here? If we can answer these questions I am sure we will be able to solve the riddle of this place.'

'It doesn't matter what we solve in here,' Bryce said. 'We are still trapped.'

'I disagree,' Watch said. 'Knowledge is power. If we can know more than Marvin, we can overpower him.' He turned to Adam. 'You're the one who can best break out of here. You have to get to Cindy, tell her that we're trapped here.'

'I have tried to walk through the walls,' Adam said. 'You saw that it didn't work.'

'I saw that you were afraid to let it work,' Watch said. 'I suspect fear is the great barrier to gaining powers in this realm. You must get over that fear and get to Cindy, and tell her the same thing. Remember, she is a fairy princess. She must have all kinds of magical powers by now.'

Adam approached the heavy metal door and shook his head uneasily.

'But what if I get stuck in the door?' he complained.

Watch came up by his side. 'You will only get stuck if you're afraid of getting stuck.'

'But that is exactly what I am afraid of!'

'I told you, you must conquer that fear,' Watch said. 'Keep reminding yourself that you're a ghost, and that you can't get hurt. Then just step through the door. If you can do it once, you'll be able to walk through anything.'

Adam went to take a deep breath before realising that he was no longer actually breathing. He wondered if that meant he was dead. It was not a pleasant thought. He closed his eyes and tried to concentrate on Casper and other friendly ghosts he knew of. When his mind was relatively calm, he took a long step forward. Behind him he heard the others gasp with pleasure. When he opened his eyes and turned around he saw that he was standing outside the dungeon.

'I did it!' he exclaimed.

'Hurry and get to Cindy,' Watch said. 'Bring her here. She should be able to open this door with her powers.' He glanced at Sally and Bryce's fangs and added anxiously, 'I don't know how long I can last here with these two characters.'

Adam nodded. 'I will find her.'

'But if you're gone too long don't blame us if we kill him,' Bryce said.

'Not that we want to kill him,' Sally added sweetly.

Their last remarks gave Adam plenty of reason to hurry. He raced back up the steps, taking two or three at a time, before he realised he didn't really need to touch the ground at all with his feet. Soon he was just flying along, passing through door after door, room after room. In a way it was kind of fun being a ghost. If he hadn't been so anxious about the vampires killing his friend, he probably would have enjoyed the sensation.

Adam eventually found Cindy sitting alone in her bedroom on the edge of her bed. She was crying quietly. Adam almost scared her to death when he flew right in front of her. She leapt up suddenly and let out a loud cry.

'Is that you, Adam?' she said, squinting. Apparently he was getting harder to see, at least in a lighted room. In the black dungeon he had glowed nicely.

'Yes, it is me. I have several important things to tell you. Marvin has locked Watch in a dungeon with Sally and Bryce. But the vampires are getting real thirsty. We have to get Watch away from them. We all have to get out of here. But you're the only one who can save us. Cindy, you have to use your magic wand.'

She held it up and waved it weakly in the air.

'I've been trying to use it for the last hour,' she said. 'I can't – nothing happens.'

'You have to believe that you can do it,' Adam said. 'And you can't be afraid. The moment I was able to do that, I was able to walk through walls. Come, take your magic wand and zap the door. Break the lock, I know you can do it.'

'OK,' Cindy said, stepping to the door. 'But I've already tried this a dozen times.'

'See it happening in your mind first,' Adam said. 'Then touch the wand to the knob. It's easy, really.'

Cindy nodded and closed her eyes and took a deep breath. She pretended for a moment that she was an all-powerful fairy, that nothing could stand in her way. Then she opened her eyes and touched the door with her wand.

The door exploded outward in a million pieces.

'Wow,' Adam said in admiration. 'You're one mean fairy. Hurry, let's rescue the others.'

Unfortunately as they raced down the steps that led to the dark dungeon, they saw that Wild Bill and Mr Green Strong-Man were guarding the passageway. Adam wanted Cindy to zap them with her wand but she was afraid of hurting them.

'Then just put a fairy sleep spell on them,' Adam said.

Cindy tried but then shook her head in distress.

'I can't do it,' she said. 'I keep worrying I'll accidentally make them explode.'

'They won't explode unless you think about them exploding,' Adam said.

'That's the problem, I can't get the idea out of my

109

mind. I tell you Adam, it won't work. My fear is blocking me.'

'Then we will have to go for other help,' Adam said. 'We can't waste time.'

'You think we should try to get back to the carnival?' Cindy asked.

'No. I think we should get back to the trapdoor, and get outside help.'

'But what if I can't blow open the trapdoor?' Cindy asked.

'Then we'll never get out of here,' Adam replied.

Eleven

Sally and Bryce had Watch cornered in the dungeon and were trying to apologise for the fact that they were about to open his veins and drink his blood.

'You know we've been friends a long time,' Sally said as she and Bryce held Watch pinned to the wall. 'We wouldn't drink your blood unless we were really desperate.'

Watch chewed on the end of his pipe, shaking. 'Can't you guys hold on a little longer? Adam should be here with Cindy any minute.'

Bryce shook his head. 'Sorry old pal. We don't think they're coming back.' He turned to Sally. 'Which vein should we open?'

'One of the neck veins will give us the most blood,' Sally said.

'But if you open my jugular or carotid,' Watch said, 'I'll die.'

'Maybe not,' Bryce said as he opened his mouth and showed his fangs. He moved in for a big bite. 'It's always possible that when we're done with you you'll turn into a vampire like us.'

Just then there was a knock at the door.

'Hey,' a familiar voice said. 'Are you guys in there?'

It as Barb, maybe Betty. Watch didn't care which one it was. He was just happy Bryce and Sally let him go and stepped to the door. The two vampires glanced at each other.

'It's the two headed lady,' Sally said.

Bryce licked his lips. 'She will have twice as many neck veins.'

'Hold on you guys,' Barb said from outside the door, and it was definitely Barb. 'I heard that. If I let you out of there you have to promise not to kill me.'

'We promise!' Watch shouted, hurrying to the door. 'Please hurry.'

The door swung open a moment later and they saw Barb and Betty standing in the dark dressed as the coachman who had driven them to the mansion. They understood now the reason he – she – had worn the huge hat. The two heads gestured to their costume.

'We were afraid Marvin would try to hurt you guys so we bummed a ride,' Betty explained.

'I had to talk her into it actually,' Barb said and glanced over her shoulder. 'We had to knock out Wild Bill and the Strong-man to get down here. They could wake any second. We have to get back to the carnival. Exciting things are happening.'

'What?' Watch asked.

'When you humiliated the Master at his magic show,' Barb explained, 'a lot of us old hands wondered if his powers were waning. All of a sudden several people began to remember that they have not always been captive here. People started talking about the past, bringing back old memories. The last I heard the whole carnival was moving towards the old trapdoor. They want out of here.'

'Then that's where we must go,' Watch said. 'But have you seen our friends – Adam and Sally?'

Barb and Betty both shook their heads.

'We have no idea where they are. All we know is that Marvin is going to try to head off the mob at the trapdoor. But I still have the stage coach waiting outside. We might be able to beat him there.'

Sally complained. 'But I need some human blood.'

'So do I,' Bryce grumbled and glanced once more at Watch.

Watch quickly stepped out of the prison.

'Barb, Betty,' he said. 'Do you mind if I ride up front with you?'

Twelve

The auditorium at the base of the wooden stairs that led up to the trapdoor was jam packed. The whole carnival was there. Watch and the vampires saw Cindy and Adam as well as they raced in on their stage coach. Watch hugged Cindy – and tried to hug Adam – he was so happy to see them both. But Bryce and Sally just stared at the crowd and licked their lips and muttered among themselves about their thirst and other bloody things. Watch pointed to the stair-way and addressed the whole crowd.

'We have to get up this way!' he shouted. 'And get out of here before Marvin arrives!'

The crowd cheered.

But suddenly there was a loud explosion.

The stairway was engulfed in smoke and fire.

When it cleared a dark figure was standing there.

Marvin stood above them, on the stairs.

He looked angry and he looked powerful.

'No one leaves here without my permission!' he yelled. 'You are my slaves! Get back to the carnival or I will kill you all!'

Cindy climbed to the first step. 'Hurt one of them and I will never help you!'

Marvin laughed bitterly. 'You think you can threaten me? You will do my bidding. This is my realm and I am all-powerful here. If you do not open the trapdoor, I will kill one of your friends.' And he pointed a dangerous finger at Watch.

'If you are so powerful,' Adam said. 'Why do you need her help?'

'Shut up!' Marvin howled, and he looked crazed. 'Or I will destroy you as well.'

'I think Adam is already pretty destroyed,' Sally muttered.

'Silence!' Marvin screamed, turning back to Cindy. 'Now do what I say this moment or one of your friends dies.'

Cindy looked anxiously from Marvin to Watch.

'What am I supposed to do?' she cried.

Bryce rubbed his hands together and spoke to Sally.

'If someone dies soon we will finally get something to drink,' he said.

'We have to drink their blood as they die,' Sally reminded him. 'Or else we will get indigestion.'

Watch stepped forward. He actually stepped up three steps in Marvin's direction, passing Cindy on the stairway. He stared at Marvin a moment and then shook his head.

'Marvin,' he said softly. 'Even if Cindy is able to blow open the trapdoor, I don't think you can just walk out of this place.'

Marvin's face trembled but then he mastered himself and sneered.

'That's not true!' he shouted. 'I made this place! I can leave when I wish!'

'Obviously that is not true,' Cindy said. 'Marvin, listen to Watch. He is a master at solving mysteries, even when he is not dressed up like Sherlock Holmes.'

Marvin paused, uncertain. 'Speak,' he finally said to Watch.

Watch gestured overhead. 'There is a ghost waiting up there in your old house, Marvin. Did you know that?'

Marvin trembled. 'What ghost?'

'It is not *what* ghost,' Watch explained. 'It is *whose* ghost.'

Marvin continued to shake. 'I don't understand.'

'But you should understand,' Watch said in a gentle tone. 'It was your house where we saw the ghost. It was in fact in your bedroom that we heard him cry.' He paused. 'Do you understand me, Marvin?'

But the great magician had turned as pale as a ghost.

'There is nothing to understand,' he said anxiously. 'You're making this up!'

The pieces finally came together for Cindy. She took a step closer to Marvin.

'What Watch is saying is true, Marvin,' she said. 'You remember how you told me how sick you got? How you used the witch's magic to make yourself better? Well you didn't really make yourself better.'

Marvin shook his head faintly. 'No. This can't be. It isn't true.'

Watch spoke with compassion. 'It is true. The ghost upstairs belongs to you. It is waiting for you, to take you to the other side. It is your ride to that place, you might say. But when you tried to cheat death by using magic, you got trapped here. Since then the ghost has been bringing you people, but they all ended up getting trapped here as well. This entire realm, Marvin, is just some place stuck between the living and the dead. That's why no one ages here. But all the people that did get trapped here, with the exception of you – we don't belong here.' Watch paused and drew out the old magic book from his back pocket. 'You have to let us go, Marvin. And you have to get together with your ghost and go on.'

But Marvin was consumed with terror.

'You lie!' he shouted. 'I can't be dead! I am too powerful. I am the world's greatest magician!' He raised a deadly hand. 'I can kill you with a flick of my finger!'

Cindy jumped in front of Watch. 'Marvin! Don't! He's trying to help you!'

'I would like to help you,' Watch said as he held the book of magic close to his smoking pipe. 'I would like the decision for you to go on to the other side to be yours alone. But if you don't release us, I will set this book on fire. It will burn and your magic will be destroyed. You were never that great a magician, Marvin. Someone else gave you this book, and I suspect it is the source of all your power. Am I right?'

'Madeline Templeton gave it to him,' Cindy said quickly.

Watch practically put a corner of the book in the pipe.

The pages began to smoke, to spark.

Marvin let out a desperate cry. 'Stop!' It was almost as if he too had begun to burn, his face looked so red and full of blood. He sweated feverishly. Watch removed the book from the fire while Marvin glanced anxiously overhead. Then the great magician lowered his head in shame and fear. 'Is it really waiting for me?' he asked.

Cindy moved up to where he was standing and put her arm around Marvin.

'It is waiting for you, yes,' she aid. 'But it is not a mean ghost. He is just lonely. He needs you to go and you need him. It is like you have been torn in two all these years, Marvin, down here in this horrible place. I am sure that when you were a young boy practising your magic you never thought of hurting people with your tricks.'

Marvin looked at her with tears in his eyes. 'That is true. I only wanted to use magic to make people laugh.' He stared out over his gathered audience. They stared at him in wonder, as if they were seeing him for the first time. Not as some mean master but just as a frightened boy who was afraid of what was happening in his sick body. A shudder went through Marvin and he slowly nodded his head as he wiped his tears. He added, 'It was not right, what I did. It is not right what I have been doing.'

Watch came up the steps and squeezed his arm.

'It is all right to make a mistake,' he said. 'Just don't keep making the same mistakes. Let these people go. Let yourself go on. We can walk up the steps together. We can introduce you to your ghost. Like Cindy said, he is not such a bad fellow.'

'You might find it will be like meeting an old friend,' Cindy said sweetly.

Marvin finally smiled faintly and hugged them both.

'You are my friends,' he said with feeling. 'You have saved me from myself.'

Down below Sally turned to Bryce.

'I think when we get out of here we won't be craving blood any more,' she said.

Bryce nodded. 'It's a shame in a way. We'll never know what it tastes like to a vampire.'

Sally grinned and showed her fangs. 'But I bet it tastes good.' Then she suddenly frowned. 'But maybe when we're human again we would be really grossed out that we drank it. No, Bryce, I think this way is better. And Cindy would never have let us live it down if we had killed Watch.'

'I should say,' Cindy muttered as she lifted up her magic wand and started up the stairs. The gang followed; the whole carnival did.

Epilogue

Later, they were all outside the Evil House, and free of the curse, and Marvin was safely on his way to the other side with his friendly ghost. And they were having the best Halloween anyone could ever remember, with everyone from the past running around trick or treating in their old costumes, knocking on doors and getting candy. In just one night Spooksville's population had grown by over a hundred people. They even had Teddy Fender back, Wild Bill himself. He apologised for being so mean to them.

But one thing puzzled the gang. As they were strolling along the dark streets, they ran into Betty and Barb – the two headed woman. And she still had two heads.

'But we thought you only dressed up as a two headed woman,' Adam said.

They both smiled and spoke in unison. 'No. This is the way we are. We were dressed up as fortune-tellers. You didn't know?'

Adam laughed. 'What does our fortune look like now?'

Barb and Betty glanced around. 'It looks very exciting.'

Sally smiled. 'Living in this town, I can believe that.'